Y0-CAT-064

THE SKY'S THE LIMIT

MAKING GOOD DECISIONS

BY STEPHANIE FINNE

BLUE OWL
BOOKS

TIPS FOR CAREGIVERS

Social and emotional learning (SEL) helps children manage emotions, learn how to feel empathy, create and achieve goals, and make good decisions. Strong lessons and support in SEL will help children establish positive habits in communication, cooperation, and decision-making. By incorporating SEL in early reading, children will be better equipped to build confidence and foster positive peer networks.

BEFORE READING

Talk to the reader about making decisions. Explain that all decisions, good or bad, have consequences.

Discuss: What kinds of decisions do you make each day? Have you had to make a big decision? What was the first thing you did? What did you decide? How did it make you feel?

AFTER READING

Talk to the reader about a difficult choice he or she may have to make.

Discuss: What is the question or problem? What are your options? What outcomes are likely for each solution? What do you think is the best solution?

SEL GOAL

Some students may struggle with self-management, making it hard to make good decisions. They may not be able to successfully regulate their emotions, thoughts, and behaviors. Help readers develop self-management skills. Help them learn to stop and think about their feelings. How can they manage stress and control impulses? How can they motivate themselves? Discuss how learning to do these things can help them make good decisions.

TABLE OF CONTENTS

CHAPTER 1

MAKING CHOICES

We make decisions every day. Some decisions seem easy. For example, you might choose what to wear each day or what to eat for breakfast.

Other decisions are more difficult, such as choosing good friends. All decisions have **consequences**. These can be good or bad. Learning to make good decisions helps us reach positive **outcomes**.

Some decisions are made quickly.
Others take a lot of thought.
When making a big decision,
think about your **values**.
What is important to you?

Daisy asks Ben to help her cheat on a test. This is a hard decision. Why? Ben wants to help his friend. But he knows cheating is wrong. Ben decides he won't help Daisy cheat. But he will help her study. They both do well on the test!

CHAPTER 2

FIVE STEPS

There are five steps to follow to help make a decision. First, **identify** the problem. Let's say you see a friend being bullied. You want to help.

The next step is to think about possible **solutions**. List outcomes that could happen for each. Who will be affected by your decision? Standing up to the bully may make it harder for your friend. Or the bully could turn on you.

teacher

Step three is to decide if you need help. Are there any **risks** if you stand up to the bully? Are you comfortable with your options? If not, ask a trusted adult for help.

THINK ABOUT TIMING

Think about how long you have to make your decision. Should you act now or wait? Why?

The fourth step is to make your decision and act on it. You decide to ask an adult for help. The counselor helps **resolve** the issue.

CHANGING COURSE

It is normal to worry about making the wrong choice. If your outcome did not solve the problem, try another option. If that doesn't work, gather more information. You can make a new decision and try again.

counselor

The final step is to **reflect** on your decision. Was it a positive outcome? You were **mindful** in your decision. Talking to the school counselor felt right. The bullying stopped. Your friend was happy for your help.

CHAPTER 3

MINDFUL DECISIONS

Sometimes decisions don't work out. Tenley decided to stay out after dark. She broke her parents' rules. They **grounded** her for a week. Now she knows what the consequences are. Every decision is a chance to learn.

Not everyone will agree with your decisions. Different people have different values. Try to find an option that is best for everyone.

Making decisions can be **stressful**. One way to make mindful decisions is to practice STOP:

Stop what you are doing.

Take a deep breath.

Observe what is happening with your body, **emotions**, and mind.

Proceed to make an **intentional** choice.

FEELING STRESS

It is OK to feel **frustrated** or cry. Making decisions can be hard. So can living with the consequences of your decisions. But making a mistake or wrong choice helps us learn for next time. Reflect and work through your feelings.

Think about how each decision you make affects others. What do your decisions mean to your family, friends, and community? Choose to be kind and mindful in all decisions!

GOALS AND TOOLS

GROW WITH GOALS

Making good decisions can be hard. But when you do what feels right, it feels great! You can work on making good decisions.

Goal: Think about what you want to achieve. What goals do you have? What decisions can help you reach those goals?

Goal: Be aware of how your decisions affect others. Think about your friends and family. Will any of your decisions hurt them?

Goal: Be flexible. Just because you make a decision doesn't mean you can't change your mind. If something isn't working, are you willing to try another route?

TRY THIS!

Some decisions can be tricky. One way to work through a hard decision is to make a pros and cons list. Draw a line down the middle of a piece of paper to make two columns. At the top of one, write "Pros." Write "Cons" on the other. Think about the decision you have to make and a possible solution. List all good things about the solution under Pros. All negative things will go under Cons. This will help you evaluate if there are more positives or negatives to the solution you are debating.

GLOSSARY

consequences
Results of actions, conditions, or decisions.

emotions
Feelings, such as happiness, sadness, or anger.

frustrated
Annoyed or angry.

grounded
To have your activity restricted.

identify
To recognize or tell what something or who someone is.

intentional
Purposeful or deliberate.

mindful
A mentality achieved by focusing on the present moment and calmly recognizing and accepting your feelings, thoughts, and sensations.

outcomes
Results of actions or events.

reflect
To think carefully or seriously about something.

resolve
To find a solution to a problem or to settle a difficulty.

risks
Possibilities of loss, harm, or danger.

solutions
Answers or means to solving problems.

stressful
Causing mental or emotional strain or pressure.

values
A person's principles of behavior and beliefs about what is important in life.

TO LEARN MORE

FACT SURFER

Finding more information is as easy as 1, 2, 3.

1. Go to www.factsurfer.com

2. Enter "**makinggooddecisions**" into the search box.

3. Choose your book to see a list of websites.

INDEX

Blue Owl Books are published by Jump!, 5357 Penn Avenue South, Minneapolis, MN 55419, www.jumplibrary.com

Copyright © 2021 Jump! International copyright reserved in all countries. No part of this book may be reproduced in any form without written permission from the publisher.

Library of Congress Cataloging-in-Publication Data

Names: Finne, Stephanie, author.
Title: Making good decisions / Stephanie Finne.
Description: Minneapolis: Jump!, Inc., 2021. | Series: The sky's the limit | Includes index. | Audience: Ages 7–10
Identifiers: LCCN 2020028301 (print) | LCCN 2020028302 (ebook)
ISBN 9781645278528 (hardcover)
ISBN 9781645278535 (paperback)
ISBN 9781645278542 (ebook)
Subjects: LCSH: Decision making–Juvenile literature. | Self-confidence–Juvenile literature. | Attitude (Psychology)–Juvenile literature.
Classification: LCC BF448 .F56 2021 (print) | LCC BF448 (ebook) | DDC 153.8/3–dc23
LC record available at https://lccn.loc.gov/2020028301
LC ebook record available at https://lccn.loc.gov/2020028302

Editor: Jenna Gleisner
Designer: Anna Peterson

Photo Credits: SLP_London/iStock, cover; Nattawun/iStock, 1; Victor Moussa/Shutterstock, 3; all_about_people/Shutterstock, 4; Prostock-studio/Shutterstock, 5; mediaphotos/iStock, 6–7; Wavebreakmedia Ltd/Dreamstime, 8; digitalskillet/iStock, 9; kali9/iStock, 10–11; SDI Productions/iStock, 12–13; wavebreakmedia/Shutterstock, 14–15; Peter Berglund/iStock, 16; JackF/iStock, 17; cheapbooks/Shutterstock, 18–19; Noriko Cooper/Dreamstime, 20–21.

Printed in the United States of America at Corporate Graphics in North Mankato, Minnesota.